THE WORST BREAKFAST

BY CHINA MIÉVILLE
& ZAK SMITH

To Cassia
—China Miéville

To all the picky eaters. It gets better, I promise.
—Zak Smith

China Miéville is the author of numerous books, including *The City & The City*, *Embassytown*, *Railsea*, and *Perdido Street Station*. His works have won the World Fantasy Award, the Hugo Award, and the Arthur C. Clarke Award (three times). He lives and works in London.

Zak Smith is an artist who first came to prominence with his mammoth work *Pictures Showing What Happens on Each Page of Thomas Pynchon's Novel Gravity's Rainbow*. Smith's paintings and drawings are held in major public and private collections worldwide, including the Museum of Modern Art and the Whitney Museum of American Art. He lives and works in Los Angeles and tries to answer all of his mail.

Artwork photographed by Cary Whittier

Printed in China by RR Donnelley Asia
Production Date: May 2016
Plant Location: No. 47 Wuhe Nan Road, Bantian Ind. Zone
Shenzhen, PRC

ISBN: 978-1-61775-486-9
Library of Congress Control Number: 2016935094
First printing

Black Sheep/Akashic Books
232 Third Street, Suite A115
Brooklyn, NY 11215, USA
Twitter: @AkashicBooks
Facebook: AkashicBooks
E-mail: info@akashicbooks.com
Website: www.akashicbooks.com

You can't have forgotten the worst breakfast!
The toast was burnt. The SMELL!
The SMOKE! It made us CHOKE!

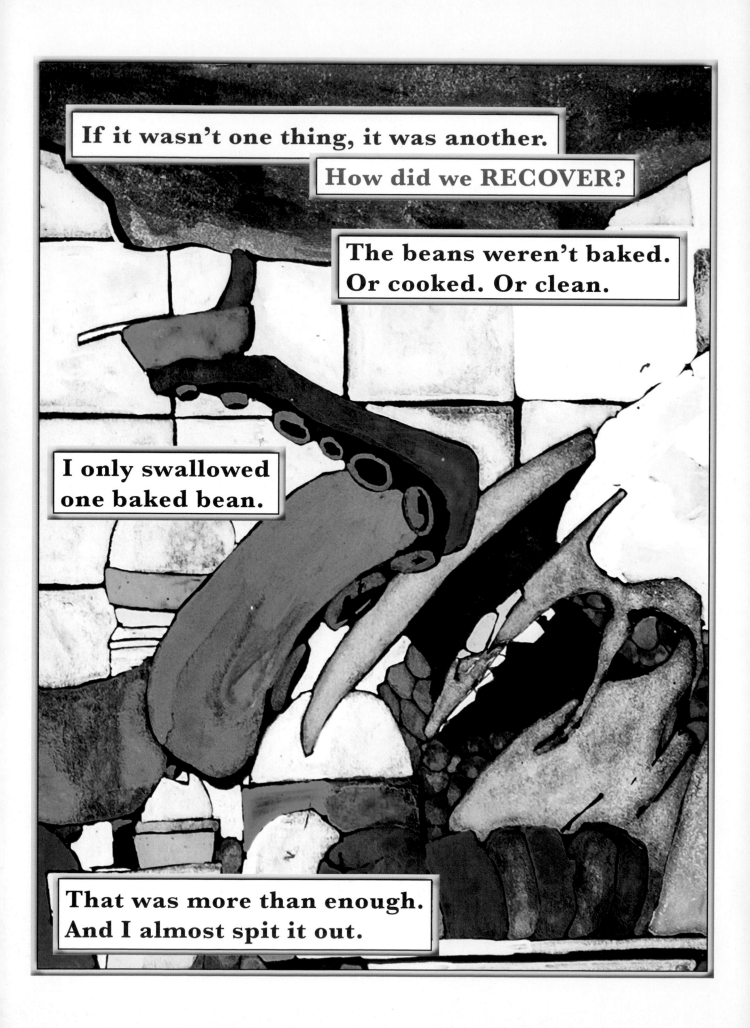

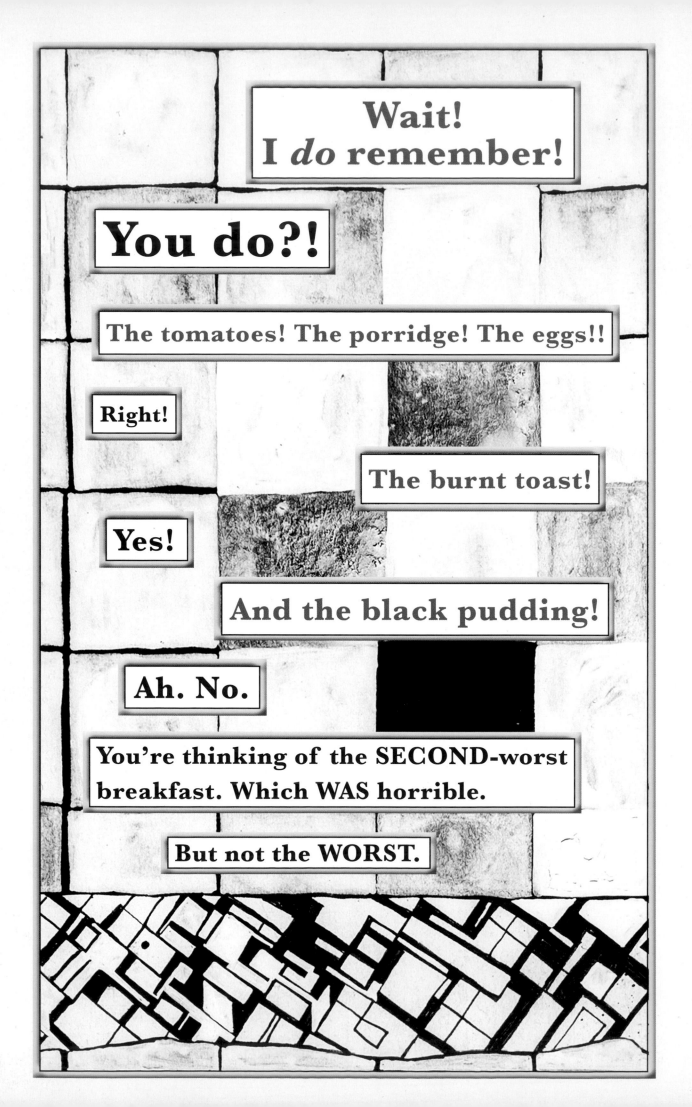

I don't remember there ever being *that* much honey for breakfast. Anyway, I like honey.

I like honey too. But not on everything. Not on bacon. And anyway, the bacon was just gross.

How can I get this through to you? It tasted like a **DEEP-FRIED SHOE.**

Surely you remember?
There was so much food. And it was HIDEOUS.

There were crumpets and marmalade and bubble-and-squeak, biscuits in clam juice, kedgeree that *reeked*. Kickshaw, flummery, plum sauce, and yarg. Jellied eels and toad-in-the-hole, pigs-in-a-blanket and beets in a bowl.

Rarebit and suet, cracklings and tripe. Drop scones and cobbler and mice-on-a-knife. Stotties and stovies, treacle, tatties, and neeps. And stargazy pie. And rumbledethumps. And roly-poly pudding.

THERE WAS MARMITE.

No, there was VEGEMITE! And barm cakes and piccalilli and kippers. Forcemeat and grits and tuna fish flippers.

Salmagundi, gruel, stinking bishop, and liver. Scrapple and blue Stilton, scuppernong, syllabub, muktuk, and limpin' Susan. Corn dogs and warthogs, salty mash and succotash.

And ortolan. And casu marzu. And blenshaw . . . in a bap.

There was skunk and mother's meat pie. Bananas and hog hearts called love in disguise. There was cullen skink, crumbcake, cheesy mac, and devils-on-horseback. Angel's hair, candy floss, cotton candy, and ribs. Cow's fleas and cocoa nibs, weaselface and warts, with raspberry tortes. There were Reubens, priest choker, and baked Alaska. And plovers wrapped in sticking plaster.

IT WAS A DISASTER.

But it's
pretty good.